A COUNTRY FAR AWAY

Story by
NIGEL GRAY

Pictures by
PHILIPPE DUPASQUIER

ORCHARD BOOKS · NEW YORK

Orchard Books, A division of Franklin Watts, Inc.
387 Park Avenue South, New York, NY 10016

Manufactured in the United States of America
Book design by Mina Greenstein
The text of this book is set in 20 pt. Garamond No. 3.
2   4   6   8   10   9   7   5   3   1

Library of Congress Cataloging-in-Publication Data
Gray, Nigel. A country far away / story by Nigel Gray; pictures by
Philippe Dupasquier. — 1st American ed.   p.   cm.
Summary: Side-by-side pictures reveal the essential similarities between the
lives of two boys, one in a western country, one in a rural African village.
ISBN 0-531-05792-5. ISBN 0-531-08392-6 (lib. bdg.)
ISBN 0-531-07024-7 (pbk.)
[1. Manners and customs—Fiction.]   I. Dupasquier, Philippe, ill.
II. Title.   PZ7.G7813Co   1989   88-22360   CIP   AC

A COUNTRY FAR AWAY

Today was an ordinary day. I stayed home.

I helped my mom and dad.

They were pleased.

Today was the last day of school before vacation.

We went home early.

I went bike riding with my friends. I'm one of the best riders.

My mom had a baby. We can't decide what to call her.

Today it rained—so we went swimming.

Today we went into town to do some shopping.

I thought we were never going to get there.

We had to get many things. It was fun.

Then we had a celebration for my baby sister.

We had our photograph taken.

Today we played soccer. I scored a goal.

My cousin came to visit. We stayed up late.

Today I looked at some pictures of a country far away.

I'd like to go there someday…

…and make a friend.